A Fragment of Time

Avril Smith

A Fragment of Time

A Fragment of Time
ISBN 978 1 76041 494 8
Copyright © Avril Smith 2018
Cover image: Deposit Photo

First published 2018 by
Ginninderra Press
PO Box 3461 Port Adelaide 5015
www.ginninderrapress.com.au

Contents

Dedication

A Love Poem for Hugh

Dear one

I am sending you
a hug
while sitting
on that patch of sand
we named our own
hearing the waves
ceaselessly call
your name

A hug

Summer-breeze warm
the curved loop
of memory
etched in recall
sharpened through separation
blurred by tears

Dear one

I am sending you
a hug
gift of love
returned.

A Fragment of Time

I named them the Fiorelli sisters. Cora and Flora. They arrived in a closed carriage decorated by a line of tiny bells so that every movement was accompanied by music.

A dreamy child suffering from the effects of rheumatic fever, I was confined to the old nursery from which I had a perfect view of the nearest mansion half hidden by an avenue of elms.

New Year 1910 had been a time of celebration downstairs but the adults' fear of infection meant I had spent it alone. Cora and Flora became my daily companions.

Flora spent every morning resting on the garden terrace until Cora, in a somewhat severe blouse and skirt, appeared laden with refreshments on a silver tray.

The early afternoon seemed to be occupied in perfecting the dance.

Flora, a dream in coffee-coloured lace, drifted up and down the terrace in time to the music of Cora's violin. Entranced, I watched every movement, here was perfection.

Three or four times a week, towards evening, I noticed a well dressed gentleman moved cautiously through the shrubbery towards the house. His arrival seemed to be a signal for the carriage to appear.

Before long, the music of the bells drifted across the intervening space. Comings and goings as seen from the nursery window were constant.

Unanswered questions tangled with my imagination. Were Cora and Flora dancers from some far away country? Why had they hidden themselves in the old mansion? Who was their evening visitor? Why did he need to arrive in secret? My questions remained unanswered.

A week later, the morning routine came to an unexpected end when Flora lost her balance and fell. It was some time before she staggered inside on Cora's arm.

I never saw the Fiorelli sisters and their secretive visitor, or heard the music of the closed carriage again.

Pronounced recovered, I rejoined the family. Memory of my imagined companions faded.

*

2010

Baron Hill Daily

The remains of a newborn infant have been uncovered in the grounds of the old mansion on Elm Street when it was recently demolished.

The Ironbark Demolition Squad

Georgie Driscoll, the big boss, owner of the squad, was the valley's popular bachelor. It was understandable. Tall, lean, silver-haired and dimpled, George was almost always forgiven his many peccadilloes.

Mind you, he had some close shaves. There was the time he was taken with Ann Manner, the local checkout chick. Could have been a nasty bust-up there, only Ann's old man got a better job and they moved to the city.

It wasn't that Georgie was a troublemaker. We, in the valley, knew he couldn't help himself.

There were five of us in the squad. Brothers. Georgie was the eldest and smartest. He went to the city and got his demolition licence. We looked after the machinery. I was in charge of the cherry picker. Demolition squad sounds destructive but we recycled most of the leftovers.

Georgie changed tactics after Ann. He concentrated on city girls. We realised this when profits from the squad began to lessen and we all had to have a cut in our take-home pay. Georgie was apologetic. We understood, though the missus had a few hard words to say about my brother.

When we got the job to demolish the old butter factory, we didn't realise Georgie was to get himself into a situation that in a way solved everyone's problems.

If we won a contract, my brother went ahead and booked our accommodation. We thought there had been a hold-up in the motel business when he was away for more than a week.

I was busy ordering the trucks to carry our working

equipment so it was a day or two before I realised my brother was not himself. I did remark on the fact that Georgie appeared more tired than usual when he returned.

We should have realised something was brewing when he spent the next two days dozing in his office chair. He was unusually silent when tackled on the subject.

I determined to wait for an answer but it was after arriving at the motel that the truth became apparent. Georgie, once again, was in love.

The Retreat Motel was new to the valley as was the manager. Jeanie Angus was middle-aged, curved and comfortable. She laughed often, never became impatient in any situation. Her silver curls were a halo for her blue eyes and ready smile.

Georgie was her slave from the beginning. This was hard for us, as he had always been a decent boss and pulled his weight. I pointed out to my brothers that Georgie's love affairs were usually short-lived but the weeks turned into a month without change.

Things came to a head the day I went to ask Georgie's advice about an oil leak in the cherry picker. He was nowhere to be found.

In the end, I asked Jeanie, who pointed to my brother on the ride-on mower. He waved from the distance.

I was not at all surprised when Jeanie replied with a call of, 'Well done, darling.'

I realised this was very different from Georgie's other adventures when, later that evening, he took me aside.

'I've grown tired of city girls. All sharp edges, money-hungry, demanding. I'm lucky to have you in the squad, Jim. You know the ins and outs of the business from top to bottom.' He leant toward me and smiled. 'Jeanie is so comfortable, so understanding.'

It was then that I stopped worrying about my brother. I

returned to the unusually empty makeshift office, shut the door and set off to take charge of our demolition operation. I found this surprisingly easy.

The money side of the business was not a problem. Georgie's expenses were mostly for chocolates and flowers. We worked without hindrance; the weather was fine and within another month we were almost ready to depart.

The bombshell, when it came, was not entirely unexpected.

Georgie appeared at smoko and told us, 'I'm giving up the squad to help Jeanie run the motel. There's to be a wedding. Jeanie wants it to be beside the river. The motel will be closed for the week.' He looked us over. 'The squad will continue with one small change: Jim will be in charge.'

Georgie had solved his problem, trusting me enough to take charge after going to the city for my demolition licence.

'I'd like the ceremony to be at sunset.' Jeanie clasped Georgie's hand and smiled. 'If it's not too much trouble.'

'You'll have whatever you want, my darling girl.' He thought for a moment. 'It'll be easy enough to organise. I'll put out the invitations. We can hire a marquee. Jim, you contact the CWA. They can do the catering. Borrowing some chairs from the Sallies is easily done.' He pointed towards me as he moved toward his ute. 'Before I forget: we're going to need a couple of portaloos. I'll leave that up to you to organise, Jim. Make sure they're a fair distance away from the celebrations.'

The weather couldn't have been kinder for the big day. I managed to recycle a small table and a fancy arch for the ceremony. The portaloos arrived in the afternoon and were set up behind a stand of gums. Hand-painted signs on pieces of recycled timber finished the job.

Jeanie, aglow with anticipation, waited beneath the arch.

Minutes ticked by but there was no sign of Georgie. I began to feel anxious while the guests eased the waiting with ribald remarks. Had my brother decided that marriage was not for him?

Jeanie began to feel the strain after half an hour. 'Something has happened to hold him up. Could have had an accident. You need to search. I'll wait here for him.'

I was inclined to agree after I noticed Georgie's ute, polished and shiny, waiting for the bridal couple.

The shadows were long when one of Jeanie's young relatives came running up shouting, 'I've found him. He's in trouble.'

He was in real trouble. Trapped in the portaloo. Apparently he had been making a last inspection when the door, caught in a sudden gust of wind, slammed shut and remained shut no matter how he pushed and shoved. By the time we managed to find a couple of torches (in the rush of organising, I had forgotten to order lighting for the portaloo), most of the wedding guests had arrived on the scene, all ready with helpful suggestions to rescue Georgie.

It was Billy, number five in the family, who suggested we use the heavy branch of a fallen tree as a rammer to loosen the lock. Georgie was warned of our intentions and urged to huddle in the corner away from danger.

Everything would have worked to plan if there hadn't been so many helpers. The rammer got up enormous speed and weakened the lock but the portaloo slid through the grass, rolling over twice before coming to a lopsided stop. It took the best part of an hour to hose Georgie down.

We had an extra problem regarding his wedding attire. His clothes were now at the motel.

'I'll wear whatever you can find,' gasped Georgie through spurts of cold water. He pointed to me. 'Get a move on. Jeanie'll be tired of waiting.'

He need not have worried.

'I knew you'd come when you could.' She held out her arms.

'Pull up another chair. We'll be married sitting down. You can tell me later what happened.' She leant forward and patted his knee. 'I'm just glad to see you, my darling.'

The ceremony went off without a hitch. Georgie, in a pair of old trackies, a paint-spattered T-shirt and a guest's second-best work boots made his vow through swollen lips, peering with rapidly blackening eyes to place the ring on Jeanie's finger.

She embraced Georgie carefully before climbing into the ute. 'It was worth the wait,' she called as she drove them away.

I heaved a sigh of relief. The demolition squad would carry on as usual and my brother had found at last that for which he had been searching.

Introducing Mr Percival

Mr Percival was exactly one year old when he had his first unlucky meeting with a dog. It bumped against his pram, just as he was in the act of showing his nurse how he could stand up in it by himself. The combination was disastrous – Mr Percival had tumbled out head first, onto the pavement. From that moment, he was anti big dogs. They were all his enemies.

Cedric Percival grew up small and self-effacing, unwilling to offend anyone. He suffered severely from nightmares until he was eight years old. They disappeared as if by magic when the boy next door gave him a small white mouse named Mimi. If he had done so with an ulterior motive, he had been sadly disappointed. His erstwhile victim had not run screaming but had accepted the small soft scrap joyfully. It lived in his pocket, receiving all the love and affection which Mr Percival possessed in an abundance.

For fifty years, he nursed in secret his fear of big dogs and his love of mice, then came the day when he was freed at last to live his own life.

It all began with a dog, a great clumsy Labrador which bumped his arm and caused him to spill his tea all over his daughter's second-best tea cloth. Shuddering inwardly, he faced the cold fact that he would have to be moving again as he surreptitiously mopped up the spreading stain. Too late: he could feel Phyllis breathing down the back of his neck; a cold warning.

Phyllis Percival kept her temper with a superhuman effort. Heavens above, how she felt like shouting and raging. She had tried it once before and the result had not been as she had intended; she had been left feeling like a criminal while her father had slunk abjectly out of the room. Coming back to the cloth, her mind was still on her problem. Dad would have to go to June's for a long stay. Her patience was at an end. If only he would listen to her. What he needed was someone to look after him. She remembered her mother ordering his days: do this, do that. He had never seemed to have any go himself.

Phyllis shrugged. Being ordered around was completely foreign to her nature; she was the one who did the ordering. Savagely she wiped away the last signs of dampness. Even though he hated the city, Dad would have to go to June's. Perhaps he would be able to find a room down there, then he need not return. Her mouth tightened as her gaze travelled around her lounge; she was not going to stand any more breakages or accidents in her beautiful modern house. She would have sat in stunned disbelief if she had known that her father regarded the whole house as a museum: cold and cheerless.

Phyllis spent a busy hour on the phone the next morning finalising arrangements. Mr Percival recognised each argument as it was presented. Sentences like 'the change would do him good', 'it would be nice to see the grandchildren', 'he needs to mix with more people' did not help. The last was a new method of attack: his blood pressure rose with his apprehension. What could she mean? What were they up to now?

Mr Percival became thoughtful: thirty years of living with three domineering females had meant that he had had to practise many small subterfuges, not out of spite but as a sop to his ego – secretly he despised the weak-kneed character who was himself; any flattering remarks he could think of all came about twenty-four hours too late. Now, like a parcel, he was to be sent off again…

Mr Percival spent some time in the local pet shop before he approached June's house. He had walked from the station, as funds were low, so he was late, hot and tired. The thought of running away anywhere crossed his mind but he was too late. June came through the French windows, took his arm and marched him indoors.

Of the three people in his life, June was the most commanding. She was what is classed as a fine figure of a woman. Her spirit knew no reverses – she just did not recognise them as such; they were only another obstacle to be surmounted. She had approached the problem of her father characteristically. The solution did not seem too difficult: her father needed to remarry. She had run over the list of her friends who might be suitable and had come up with two possibles. Rose Lancaster was ideal, well off, recently widowed. She adopted a clinging ineffectual air toward any member of the opposite sex. Diana Cox was the other. Successful dress designer, wealthy, on the lookout for a husband.

Mr Percival's brow furrowed as he approached the tea table. Their plan came to him in a flash: he was to be pushed into taking one of these females out, 'view mat'. The thought was enough to make his knees quake; he answered the introductions absent-mindedly as the realisation of the plan became clear. Some last spark of willpower remained; bending down, he placed his latest acquisition on the floor. The effect was instantaneous. Rose screamed and jumped on to her chair. It creaked alarmingly; beneath her flowing draperies was good solid flesh. Diana jumped up and acted quickly. She whipped off her shoe and threw it. Her aim was deadly: the mouse lay in a huddled heap on the floor.

'Get out, you murderess,' he hissed, 'and you,' turning his rage onto the almost hysterical Rose, 'fancy being afraid of a mouse!'

His exit was hurried but he did not forget the small still body on the floor. Slowly he bent and picked it up. He could not and would not be badgered any more; he would have to get somewhere to live away from all managing females. But how? Where?

Mr Percival's luck was right out next morning. He was detailed off to walk Rastus to the park and back again. Rastus was the worst kind of dog, a jumping up kind. His nerves began to jingle in protest. He reached the park safely or, rather, he was dragged there.

After tying Rastus to a tree, he crouched behind a leathery tamarisk and scooped out a hole in the soft earth. In it he placed the remains of the unfortunate mouse, and wept a last farewell.

Lost, alone, his future seemed to be a succession of dreary boarding houses, unappetising food, sharing the grey days of the unwanted.

A piercing shriek interrupted his train of thought. It came from the spot where he had left Rastus. Mr Percival gathered his courage and peeped round the corner. Rastus had broken free and was standing over a huddled figure on the ground. It was the end. Without thinking, he bent down and picked up the victim's handbag; with the greatest feeling of pleasure, he cracked the dog over the nose. Rastus let go and slunk away.

Mr Percival bent over the victim and recognised her immediately. It was little Miss Clent who lived in the cottage behind the post office in the district where he and Mrs Percival had spent their holidays. A memory of her cool back veranda came unbidden; it had been a pleasant resting place on the hottest of days. The honeysuckle vines had laid cool streamers of shadow across the goldfish bowls which lined the sides.

Mr Percival dipped his handkerchief in the fountain and laid it on Miss Clent's forehead. Tentatively, he felt her hand – how small and soft it was, how blue her eyes as she gazed straight into the anxious eyes of her rescuer.

'Mr Percival,' she was apologetic, 'how silly of me to be so terrified of a dog. Thank you for rescuing me. I'm afraid of dogs. 'You're very brave.'

The effect of these words on Mr Percival was miraculous. The summer sunshine shone down upon the dwarfed bud of his manhood, warming it, kindling it into life, as he gently helped her to a seat.

The Helper

Cedric Percival never ate oysters or watched a game of football. He preferred green jelly and Belgian beer.

Cedric lived in a small semi-detached cottage in Poinsettia Lane with his boon companion Lawrence. Chubby, button brown-eyed, shy Lawrence. It was accepted that Mr Percival was his spokesman.

Cedric, neat, narrow-shouldered, with an unruly lock of black hair curling over his left eye, was a popular figure, always on call to give a helping hand.

Poinsettia Lane consisted of six cottages. Mr Percival and Lawrence occupied the first. The last was empty until Maudie Fellowes moved in. Maudie looked like a china doll with her rosy cheeks, blue eyes and a halo of white curls. Appearances were deceptive, as Poinsettia Lane soon discovered.

It began with the matter of the red bin. Number 5 and 6 shared, as did 1 and 2, 3 and 4, changing over on alternate Thursdays.

'Nasty smelly thing. I'll not be having it outside my gate. Spoils the look of my picket fence,' said Maudie.

Gentle persuasion from Mr Percival fell on deaf ears. The bin remained on the verge outside number 5.

Life in Poinsettia Lane was uneventful until the matter of the Buddhist monk shattered the peace. He wandered into Poinsettia Lane one winter evening lightly clad, clutching his begging bowl. Cedric took him in, gave him a hot meal finished by a large helping of green jelly, and sent him on his way. The truth of the matter happened quite unexpectedly when number 3, a recently retired magistrate, recognised the monk as a well known con man.

Cedric was unapologetic when taken to task. 'Poor fellow was cold and hungry,' he was heard to murmur.

Poinsettia Lane shook their heads and smiled. Their Mr Percival would always lend a helping hand.

Cedric and Lawrence ran a get together barbecue every second Saturday. Poinsettia Lane drank copious cups of tea while enjoying a sausage sandwich and much chat, until Maudie arrived on the scene.

'Should be held every week, with salads and maybe a glass or two,' she winked at Cedric, 'of the real thing.'

Poinsettia Lane held its breath while Cedric offered to make the salads. They took a vote, which resulted in five to one against.

Maudie never attended another barbecue. She chose to spend her leisure time with her new laptop. She must have bought a lemon because she constantly needed help to run it. That meant frequent visits to Cedric, often nearing dinner time.

Poinsettia Lane watched as their friendly helper grew pale and thin while Maudie blossomed. They held a meeting. Number 3 suggested Poinsettia Lane took turns to protect their helper.

'A kind of vigilante,' said number 4. 'We can't be doing that.'

'Maudie would more than likely sue us for stalking,' said number 3.

The final decision was reached when number 4 suggested they keep Mr Percival so busy with odd jobs, cups of tea and a chat that there was no time to answer Maudie's everlasting demands.

Poinsettia Lane shone with new paint and manicured gardens but Maudie managed to snatch Cedric's few free hours. Poinsettia Lane shook their heads in regret. The situation was beyond their capabilities.

Three weeks later. Poinsettia Lane, as usual, neat and tidy, seemed peaceful in the Saturday sunshine. The only noticeable difference was the big FOR SALE outside number 6.

Cedric, bright and chatty, turned the sausages expertly.

Number 3, chosen as spokesman, seized his opportunity. 'Maudie left quite unexpectedly. Wonder why?' the magistrate remarked.

Cedric turned and faced his friend. 'I can help you there.' He began to place the sausages in a neat pile. 'Unfortunately, I was very involved in her departure.' He sighed. 'I introduced her to Arthur Stubbs from Swan Close. She found him very compatible.'

Number 3, senses sharpened by his years on the bench, waited.

'I'm afraid there was some unpleasantness.' Cedric touched Lawrence on the arm. 'We could put up with the fact that she very much disliked green jelly, but,' Cedric's eyes filled with tears, 'I'm afraid I swore at her and told her to leave.' He leant forward and hugged Lawrence. 'She said my mate was old and shabby,' Cedric shook his head, 'and all he was good for was the op shop.'

Mr Percival and Louisa

'A whole week of Louisa.' Cedric Percival groaned as memories of the many lost battles with his elder sister flooded in. Seen through the spectacles of childhood, they had been constant proof of his inability to cope with opinionated females. Maybe now they were both grown-up, the situation could be different. Straightening his shoulders, he closed his computer. The reflection in the wall mirror returned a rueful smile. Those many attempts to prove his point in any situation had been rarely successful.

Cedric, relaxing in his favourite armchair, warm in his dressing gown and slippers, drifting through a dream accompanied by Vivaldi, was startled awake by continuous knocking at the front door.

Louisa? Surely not. She wasn't due for two days. Someone in trouble? Perhaps he could help. Shaking himself awake, he hurried forward.

'Surprise. Surprise,' boomed Louisa.

Cedric, smothered by a flurry of scarves, struggled ineffectually against the grip of a surprisingly strong pair of arms. Louisa, releasing her brother, strode indoors.

'Surprise indeed. I was expecting you at the weekend.'

'Business deal was concluded earlier than expected. Successfully.' She turned towards the small figure as she unwound the last scarf.

'You're looking well,' Cedric managed to gasp.'

'Can't say the same for you.' Louisa frowned beneath her black fringe as she moved suddenly toward the window and flung it open.

Cedric shuddered as a blast of freezing air filled his lungs.

'Nothing like fresh air.' She stood before the open window

breathing deeply. 'You don't know how lucky you are away from city pollution.'

Cedric began to sneeze in the middle of the night. Morosely, he counted twenty-six before Louisa in a summer nightdress swept in to hurl up his bedroom window.

'Need to blow away those germs.'

Cedric held his bedclothes in a vice-like grip until she closed the door before snuggling down so low that only his nose was visible. Coward that he felt himself to be, closing the window was impossible.

Cedric, sneezing and coughing, retired to bed for several days.

Louisa fed him regularly a weak stew, the contents of which Cedric dared not ask. She, armed with a large pruning knife, spent the days getting the garden into shape between bouts of practising her martial arts.

Cedric, improved, began to look towards evening and a hot toddy when Louisa announced, 'Milk was meant for calves, not humans.'

Dream turned to nightmare. Cedric felt an unexpected surge of anger. The coughing fit which followed was so alarming that Louise said nothing when he rushed forward and slammed down the nearest window.

Louisa, who appeared so deeply affected, made no move to reopen it but led him to a chair, slapping at his back as they progressed. Cedric lay back and wiped his streaming eyes as Louisa covered him gently with a rug.

'What an attack. Reminded me of when you were a kid and I'd been told to look after you.'

Suddenly Cedric became that child, remembering the big sister, bossy and opinionated, who had sensed that he, small and vulnerable, was to be protected.

'Sorry about that. I'll go and get some milk.' She patted his knee. 'I tend to forget that everyone is different.'

Mr Percival Goes Online

'Crikey.' Cedric Percival shuddered, tightened his grip on the mobile phone. Momentarily, the supermarket shelves (he had been shopping for his neighbour in Poinsettia Lane), seemed to wobble, leaning dangerously close. The small list in his hand fell to the ground unnoticed while he struggled to cope with an anxiety which threatened to overwhelm him.

'Nominated, nominated.' The word rang in his head like the unceasing beat of a drum as he replied. 'I'll wait to hear the intended date.'

Cedric pocketed the phone, his thoughts whirling as he stepped forward to help an elderly shopper cross the road.

Number five in a family of ten, Cedric small and uncomplaining, often went unnoticed in the general rush and bustle of everyday life until he was old enough to stack the dishwasher. It took three separate attempts before he was satisfied.

'Well done.' Kathleen Percival gently smoothed her son's hair with the palm of her hand. Now I have a full-time helper.'

Cedric threw back his head and smiled, unable to explain the pleasure those neatly stacked utensils produced, doubled when he took them, now shining clean from the machine.

Somewhat lost in the melée of his siblings, needing peace, unnoticed, he spent long hours alone, until, as a young adult, he entered a new world of computers. He bought his seventh and his mother her first, at the same time offering to help solve any difficulties she might have with her birthday gift.

Kathleen, an efficient people person, rose quickly to the

challenge and soon was looking for another project. One was not hard to find.

Some weeks later, she introduced Cedric to the first of her many friends who were struggling with their latest acquisition.

Cedric, kind and patient, now spent most of his daylight hours in a new world of the elderly. Unnoticed, a thin film of dust began to cover his late companions, while the dishwashing machine was often on the point of choking.

While Cedric looked after his harem of elderly ladies, they were spending time in quiet discussion: how could they show him their appreciation? A luncheon, chocolates, his favourite Belgian beer were all rejected. The matter was at a standstill until Kathleen produced the newspaper publicity for the Shire Citizens of the Year. Cedric's nomination was completed to whole-hearted applause.

Six weeks later, they heard they had been successful.

Sleeping became a time of nightmare in which Cedric saw himself as an object of derision, a small figure lost in a chanting mob of pointing gargoyles. He grew pale, with dark circles beneath his eyes. His hands, damp with anxiety, needed constant drying on the sides of his jeans. He became forgetful, suffered panic attacks, constantly mislaid his car keys.

Cedric was ushered to the front row of the packed hall. A small figure almost hidden in a collection of draped scarves occupied the seat beside him.

He half heard most of the preceding speeches, flushed scarlet when his name was mentioned, constantly wiped his sweating palms, wished he was far away.

His attention was diverted when the figure beside him suddenly swayed forward. Automatically, he clutched a handful of clothing and pulled her upright.

'Thank you.' Blue eyes gazed into brown. 'I'm not much good in crowds but the family wanted to see me get my award.'

She smiled wryly. 'I'm afraid I'm a bit of a coward where all this is concerned,' she confessed. 'My medallion is actually for some of my gifts to local charities.' she whispered. 'I always hoped they would be anonymous.' She shook her head and smiled at him. 'Fainting is not an answer to my problem.'

Cedric, surprisingly, suddenly felt an easing of tension. 'I know exactly what you mean. I dread the thought of standing up in front of all these people but my friends have chosen this event to show me their appreciation of my help in solving their computer problems.'

She tapped his arm gently as she sighed. 'A tangled computer is a frequent occurrence in my day.'

Cedric turned to face her. 'Maybe I could help you.' He chuckled quietly. 'I'm not afraid of computers.'

Every morning, the sun lightens the gold of the two medallions on the table in number 1 Poinsettia Lane.

Mr Percival's Summer

'We're beginning to sag in the wrong places, old boy.' Cedric Percival waved an admonishing finger at the brown-eyed, narrow-shouldered mirror image before bending down to gingerly towel his aching knees. Looked as though jogging was off his list of good health intentions. Bicycling had come first but Mr Percival's sense of balance had proved inadequate. Two nasty falls and one near miss in traffic had been enough.

'Walking is the final option. No excuses,' he said firmly while his mirror image shuddered. It, by earlier experience, had proved more than difficult. Five of the six dwellings in Poinsettia Lane were occupied by friendly owners all ready for a chat as he approached. By the time he reached the curve outside empty number 6, it was midday, the park a too distant goal.

Cedric sighed. 'Early morning, no excuses.' He waved a decisive finger in the general direction of the mirror before pulling on his shirt.

On the second morning, Mr Percival, scarved and capped against the winter chill, carried a torch after a nasty tumble outside the empty number 6 in Poinsettia Lane.

Three days in bed to recover did nothing to weaken his resolve but after that his backpack contained a thermos of coffee and his favourite mug.

When summer mornings began to lengthen, Cedric added a small garden fork and trowel because the garden near his favourite park seat needed attention.

'I'm beginning to enjoy my morning walk. Poinsettia Lane looks a treat.' Cedric pushed his hair away from his forehead and frowned. 'Except for number 6. Been empty too long, needs a bit of looking after.' He eyed the gate, hanging drunkenly. 'Won't take me a minute to fix.'

Cedric packed a hammer and nails when he set off next morning.

In the fifth week, he noticed the clematis vine was beginning to straggle across the path. Cedric sharpened his favourite secateurs before setting out. He carried them carefully in his hand. With the fully loaded backpack, his morning walk was fast becoming a route march but he felt it was worth the effort.

It was when he stepped back to admire his handy work that he noticed the large SOLD sign.

'Let's hope any newcomer is a handyman,' he muttered (Cedric often spoke his thoughts aloud) 'and they fit in with us in Poinsettia Lane.'

At the end of the sixth week, Erica Anders, red-headed and freckled, back from her night shift, collided with Mr Percival outside number 6.

'Oh dear, I am sorry. My fault.'

'Not to worry.' Erica, brushing down her uniform, smiled at the agitated stranger as she opened the gate.

'Percival's my name. Cedric Percival. Round here I'm known as Mr P. Long-time resident of number 1.' He put down the secateurs and extended his hand. 'Welcome to Poinsettia Lane.'

Erica moved closer to the elderly man with the shy smile. 'Thank you. Number 6 is my first attempt at home ownership.' She gazed upward. 'It is pretty run-down. It was all I could afford.'

Cedric's tone was sympathetic. 'Been waiting for *you*. Needs a coat of paint, a bit of a roof job and a few extras.'

'I'll have to find a tradesman. Do you know of one?'

'Standing right beside you. That's what I did all my working life. I could help you there.'

Erica, moving through the gate, turned to face Cedric.

'It'd fill in time after my morning walk.'

'How kind. Are you sure?'

Cedric nodded vigorously.

So began the halcyon days of that summer during which Cedric Percival restored number 6 Poinsettia Lane to its former beauty.

Mr Percival and Stephan

A flutter of anxiety trembled through Poinsettia Lane when No. 6 spread the news that he was taking an overseas trip and his cottage was to become an Airbnb.

Their worst fears became personal before the month was ended when the Saturday morning get-together at No. 1, Cedric Percival's residence, was held against the raucous shouting of a figure on a skateboard using their manicured nature strips as a runway.

'Someone needs a good going over on his backside,' shouted No. 5 over the added instant barking reaction of Cedric's small brown dog.

'I'd deliver it with pleasure.' No. 4 had no need to shout, having spent his entire working life as an auctioneer. Always ready to oblige, he stood up, maybe waiting for support. 'Anyone coming?'

No. 5, shaking his head, spoke firmly. 'We'd probably be charged with assault.' He turned toward his companions. 'Hard to understand how this present situation has come about. School holidays don't help. It's a problem for his mother. She's a well spoken, hard-working single parent. She and young Stephan are here on six months' exchange. Tells me she's in the banking game.'

If No. 5 hoped to ease the situation with this information, he was doomed to failure.

'Needs a stay-at-home parent.'

'You wouldn't think anyone could cause so much trouble,' shouted No. 3.

No. 2's solving of the communal problem was received in silence.

No. 3 muttered his disgust. 'No discipline today. Don't know about these young people.' He heaved a heavy sigh. 'Everything is so different.'

Grey heads nodded agreement.

Cedric Percival waited a moment as the cause of all their trouble swept noisily past. 'We may have another option.' He spoke tentatively, his words falling into an ever widening silence, but Cedric Percival possessed a strong stubborn streak. 'Tomorrow I'll show him the local rink.'

Cedric, accompanied by his small brown dog, was passing through the gate when disaster struck.

Accompanied by a mighty noise, rushing wind, the picket fence, Mr Percival, the small brown dog, a boy and a shattered skateboard fell in a tangled heap.

Cedric attempted to rise but his ankle throbbed with pain. Breathless, unable to move, he lay on the verge watching as the boy leant over him sobbing 'Sorry, sorry,' as he made frantic efforts to move piles of fencing in order to reach the still shape of the dog.

It took some time before Cedric was able to sit up. He watched with some astonishment as the dog, now fully recovered, lay cocooned in the boy's arms.

'I've always wanted a pup but there's no room in our unit in the city where we live.'

Cedric cleared several broken pieces of wood into a small heap. 'We've a job of clearing up this mess. I'm afraid I'll need help.' Cedric grimaced as he began to hobble inside. 'Might take most of the holidays.'

'I could clear away all of the broken pieces of wood.' Stephan used one foot to push several aside as he bent to recover his skateboard.

'That would be helpful. My ankle will take a week or two to recover.' Cedric gazed at the wreck shaking his head. 'Poinsettia Lane looks a real mess.'

'I could help in another way.'

'By not using the nature strip as a runway, I hope.'

Stephan smiled somewhat guiltily. 'I won't be doing that again. That was to be a farewell run. Mum showed me the park with the rink.'

Stephan set the small brown dog back onto its feet. 'Would you let me take him for his morning and afternoon walk?'

Mr Percival looked thoughtfully. 'Come to think of it, that would go a long way toward solving a very difficult situation.'

A Taste of Chocolate

Cedric Percival's resolution weakened on the twelfth day.

He was caught unawares when No. 2 Poinsettia Lane insisted on offering him a pack of continental chocolates. It was No. 2's way of saying thank you for a helping hand with a broken drainpipe but a personal disaster for Cedric.

He held the pack close for several minutes: the taste of chocolate a bliss remembered. Automatically, he moved to open the gift, ignoring the challenge of his inner voice. Cedric's fingers seemed to have developed a mind of their own.

It was a chance reading on Facebook (Cedric was a keen user) which had led him in an attempt to test the strength of his willpower to reduce the number of his secret after-dinner chocolate splurges. Cedric Percival knew himself as a confirmed, enthusiastic addict. He had read on, ever hopeful of any handy hints to solve his problem. The idea of choosing a strategy caught his attention.

Sitting in a sea of used chocolate wrappers like a drowning man, Cedric's shoulders drooped. There seemed to be no answer to his problem. He had already tried most of those offered, and the final strategy of sucking on a matchstick when the craving threatened to overcome him had been useless. Cedric was a non-smoker.

It was No. 3 Poinsettia Lane who sold him the winning ticket. A cruise to Fiji. Cedric, exhausted by his futile efforts to cope with his addiction, had folded his three favourite shirts into his backpack dreaming of freedom. Maybe, after all, a holiday was to be his successful strategy.

Like chocolate, Cedric was addicted to his computer almost to the point of Google being his best friend. At other times, Poinsettia Lane often called on him for assistance to unwind their tangles.

His knowledge became apparent each night of the trivia competition; more so when the bulk of contestants were white-haired and given to nodding off, exhausted from taking part in the daily activities aboard. Five chocolate gifts so filled his backpack he was forced to leave his shirts behind.

On the sixth and final night of competition, Cedric was presented with a framed certificate in appreciation of his trivia skills.

Saturday morning's regular get together at No. 1 Poinsettia Lane was held soon after his return. Each guest received a pack of chocolate on leaving.

'Won them aboard. Had a bit of luck in the trivia competitions.'

'Very generous of you.' No. 3 grasped his gift firmly. He looked around at his companions. 'Sure I speak for everyone here. What about you? Got any extras stashed away? Can't say I blame you if that is so. A block or two with my evening tipple is a must.'

White heads nodded agreement.

'Afraid we're all small-time addicts.' No. 4's remark held a note of laughter as No. 6 lead a round of noisy applause.

'I've tried to cut down countless times,' mused No. 2. He smiled at his companions. 'Never give up is a worthwhile motto.'

Cedric suddenly relaxed. He was not alone. He had managed those days aboard without chocolate. Maybe it would become easier but, if he did fall by the wayside, he would be among understanding companions in Poinsettia Lane.

Mr Percival Goes on a Health Kick

Mr Percival came to a final decision while sitting on the side of his bed rubbing his aching knees. His jogging days were over. Sighing heavily, he limped, shaver in hand, towards the wall mirror from where a slight-shouldered, brown-eyed figure frowned.

'I did try,' he muttered. (Mr Percival often shared his thoughts with his reflected friend.) 'Maybe I went at it too soon, too often, too hard.' His reflection nodded.

The realisation that there was no longer a pressing need to vacate his warm bed and face the often chilly dawn (Mr P was not a group participant) was small satisfaction until it was followed by a moment of guilt as memories of those earlier attempts to follow his new health routine came flooding back.

The local gym had been his first choice but the noise and constant movement became an assault, the various machines' offerings of imminent danger against which he had no answer. Uncertain, self-conscious, he let his membership lapse.

Mr Percival eyed his reflection gloomily. He shook his head from side to side, his lips tightening as he combed his hair. A last glance into the mirror could not be denied. He was beginning to sag in the wrong places. Action was imperative. 'I'll have to try something different,' he thought as he heaved his trousers over the swelling bud of his abdomen, 'something I'd enjoy.'

Helmeted, suitably dressed and shod, Mr Percival pushed his new cycle through the gate onto the nature strip. Steadying the shiny machine with one hand, he raised his smart phone. (Mr P was a wholly converted gadget consumer.) 'Cheese, cheese' accompanied by a smile caught the moment before he began yet another health kick adventure.

Progress was slow. It was a week of wobbles, two near misses of several pedestrians which involved him in a series of apologies and left him wondering if he did need new glasses, but Mr Percival possessed a streak of determination combined with the realisation that his sense of balance was not his strong point.

A fortnight later, he managed his first trip to the park. So began that month of accomplishment during which Mr Percival's manhood blossomed as he swerved almost professionally between children and leash free dogs.

It was a small brown dog that ended those halcyon days by running directly across his path. He gazed down at the wreckage (the dog had disappeared), while flexing his arms and legs. Nothing seemed to be broken but the mangled remains of his machine were beyond repair.

'I should have known good things don't last with me,' he muttered to a cluster of would-be helpers. Needing time to recover, he limped toward the nearest bench half hidden beside a bushy tamarisk.

Shoulders slumped, helmet askew, trousers showing a large tear, Mr Percival fell into a deep depression. Twilight shadowed the park before he managed to ready himself to move. As he did so, he realised he was not alone. The small brown dog, shivering and bedraggled, cause of all his troubles, half hidden, lay almost at his feet.

Mr Percival leant down. 'Almost missed you. Sorry about that.' He eyed the small figure, speaking softly. 'We've both had a bad day.' Compassion deepened his tone. 'A very bad day.'

The softly spoken word resulted in a series of feeble tail wags. Mr Percival held out a tentative hand. The small bundle uncurled slightly before moving slowly forward. Encouraged, he bent down and took the dog in his arms.

The pup whimpered but stayed quietly when he was moved into the warmth of the bike jacket. A careful look round showed the park to be deserted.

'Time to go home.' Gently he patted the small curve of his jacket. 'Seems we were meant to be together.'

A warm tongue licked agreement.

Mr Percival's search for a more healthy life style has ended. He and his small brown dog have taken up walking.

Mr Percival's Xmas

Xmas was not a happy time for Mr Percival. 'Too many memories of those happy family gatherings,' he was heard to mutter in explanation as he close his curtains and became invisible.

The situation changed when the small brown dog became his companion.

'Can't keep you cooped up here. Let's go somewhere different today.' He bent down and patted the smooth head. 'Almost ready,' he called as he tucked the dog's drinking bowl into his backpack. 'Can't forget my mate. We've got some way to go.'

Mr Percival's world had widened since he and the small brown dog began to take a daily walk. He returned to a world very different from the ordered greenery of Poinsettia Lane, a world of wide space set above the bank of a creek shadowed by willows; the world of Mr Percival's childhood.

In the warmth of sunshine, he leant against the trunk of the largest tree recalling the feel of bark beneath his ten-year-old palms reliving that sense of achievement when the highest branch was reached. So much to remember. Times of safety and freedom as he, bare-footed, ran through the grass, thick after rain, his dog racing ahead.

Gently, he caressed the soft ears of his here and now companion lying so quietly beside him.

He was back in the homestead of his childhood feeling again that sense of anticipation, choosing and helping decorate the tree with paper chains and silver-painted pine cones gift of a tree in the home paddock.

Lost in his dream of yesteryear, he was suddenly wakened by

the sound of voices. Two young children, each with a bright new bike, were standing on the opposite bank.

'Thank you for our presents, Santa,' the smaller of the two called shrilly as he moved closer to the edge of the bank.

'We thought you might miss us this year. The drought was really bad.'

Mr Percival brushed his hand through his beard before waving to the two figures as they disappeared over the hill. 'Imagine that now.' He turned to his companion. 'I suppose there is some resemblance.'

The small brown dog stretched before licking his hand as they prepared to leave.

Mr Percival eased into his backpack, smiling thoughtfully. 'Maybe I could be a Santa next year.'

Molesy

After two years of being a victim of the bully Butch Pugh, Molesy (christened Tom) Burrowes decided to become invisible. It was difficult at first, His pale ginger fringe, snub nose and thick bifocals were not easily missed, but Molesy possessed a very stubborn streak. He hid himself in the school library and attached to his iPod (Tom was not a student), his much loved harmonica hidden in his deepest pocket, he drifted along to the sounds of his favourite music.

Crystal Flowers took a different path. She became a judo champion.

Now eighteen, they met while packing shelves in the local convenience store. It was quite a surprise when Crystal realised they had both been at the same school. Eldest of a big family, she possessed a strong motherly streak, so determined to take Tom under her wing. This was difficult. Tom ducked and weaved, but Crystal too possessed a stubborn streak

She began to feel she was getting somewhere when he accepted an extra sandwich during what became a shared lunch break.

Tom, somewhat a stranger to kindness, hid his feelings. Crystal began to occupy his daydreams. Attempts to remain invisible became erratic. Before long his iPod was abandoned. Tom was in love. He dreamt of becoming a star attraction at a big music festival accepting congratulations about his harmonica playing from an admiring Crystal while the subject of his dreaming lay awake at night planning ways to lift the burden of his loneliness.

The situation remained static for several weeks while Tom struggled to think of a gift for Crystal.

Dreams turned to nightmares when Butch re-entered their lives. He, beetle-browed, bearded, broad-shouldered, became an unwanted addition to their lunch break. No longer interested in tormenting Molesy, Crystal with her piquant face and blue eyes became his challenge. 'Wot yer doin' with a worm like 'im?' Butch extended a hairy arm, finger pointing toward a trembling Molesly. 'Piss off, you.' He blew a cloud of smoke in the direction of his late victim. 'And quick.'

The lump in Molesy's throat threatened to choke him. He wiped his sweaty palms against the sides of his jeans. Crystal, in one fluid movement stood beside Tom.

Butch smirked maliciously. 'Empty yer pockets before I decide to let yer go.' The car door slammed as he moved closer. 'What about a ride, girlie?'

Crystal ignored the supplicant while Tom's trembling became a steady shaking.

'I'd show youse a real good time.' Butch, not used to asking for anything, waited for the answer he expected.

When Crystal remained silent, his small patience evaporated. Wheedling became threat. He turned his full attention on to the hapless Tom.

Tom, harmonica in hand, moved away from Crystal, back against the wall as Butch stepped forward, arm outstretched shouting, 'I'll 'ave that, and pronto.'

Tom, tears threatening to blind him, felt a sudden surge of unexpected anger. The threat to Crystal had been torment enough; shame over his weakness in giving in so easily to Butch was the last straw. With a desperate movement, he thrust his foot forward. Butch fell heavily.

Sergeant Brand, notebook in hand, strode up the path. Butch, groaning loudly, began to struggle to his feet.

'Not you again. Parking in a loading zone twice in the one day needs more than a warning.'

With a tremendous effort, Butch staggered to his feet, prepared to run. 'Fuck yer,' he shouted as he moved forward, almost knocking over the policeman.

Crystal felt the rush of air as he was passing. With a fluid judo movement, she pinned the tormentor to the ground.

'You were so brave.' Crystal bent down to brush clean her jeans.

Tom shook his head. 'You were the brave one. I was so angry I forgot to be frightened.'

Crystal smiled as she straightened. 'We were both brave,' she giggled.

'It's hard to believe.' Tom's laughter was a celebration of freedom as they moved spontaneously towards each other and hugged.

Crystal's hand, warm and soft, lay easily in Tom's grasp as they watched the loaded van round the corner.

The Truth of the Matter?

Lachlan was dead.

Mrs Bennett, my housekeeper, handed me the letter containing the news while I was resting, enjoying the warmth of the sunshine, savouring my continual return to health. The envelope bore the stains of its six-month journey. My fingers trembled so greatly when I opened it I feared a return of my illness. The covering note from a London solicitor contained the news I dreaded. The puzzle regarding the welfare of my identical twin was now solved.

Grief overwhelmed me. Lachlan, my other half, gone from me. The words blurred through my tears as I began to read.

3 March, 1830
Sorrow at the unexpected passing of your brother was eased somewhat by the knowledge that his marriage, though of such short duration brought him great happiness.

That Ruth's death was too great a grief to bear, I consider, as did the coroner, the truth of the matter of his self-destruction.

I struggled to read the remaining sheets.

My dear brother,
I am setting down events as they occurred, hoping you will understand the truth of the matter.

Devastated as I was over the death of my beloved Ruth, I felt I had a responsibility regarding the welfare of her daughter Myfanwy. Ruth spoke of her as her little changeling. This was easy to understand as she was as dark as Ruth was fair but instead of warmth a coldness emanated from her. I sensed it from our first meeting. She left me feeling drained and fearful when we were together.

I had some understanding of her antipathy. Ruth had been hers for many years. Maybe I was at fault, being completely engrossed in savouring the realisation. I had moved out of the shadow of loneliness in to the light of loving and being loved.

Mellowed by my new-found happiness, I felt I could easily love Ruth's daughter but at our first meeting I had been taken aback by the ice-cold feel of her flesh.

I stifled a twinge of regret at this inauspicious beginning but decided given time all would be well.

Time, time to adjust. Even Brutus, boon companion of my bachelor, days slunk in to a far corner whenever she was near.

Dear brother, I swear to you I made every effort to like and be liked. In contrast, I achieved a sense of constant frustration as I beat against a wall of glass from behind which Myfanwy kept watch.

Ruth's pregnancy brought another problem. Our evening pattern changed. She retired early, so I brought much of my city affairs home. Absorbed in correspondence, time passed unnoticed until some sixth sense alerted me to the fact that I was no longer alone.

Myfanwy, black eyes shadowed, faced me. Naturally, I wished to suggest she retire but my voice was lost, stifled in my throat.

Can you believe that I became a prisoner of her gaze, without will, held as helplessly as any insect impaled by a pin?

From thence, a strange weakness began to affect me.

The page fluttered from my hand. Lachlan was describing the illness which had plagued me for so long and from which I was only now recovering. 'My poor brother,' I groaned aloud. So much so that Mrs Bennett came running to enquire if I needed assistance.

I read on with mounting apprehension.

Sharing a bed with my love remained a circumstance to be treasured until Ruth decided otherwise. I mourned this loss for some time before deciding to return to seek the comfort of Ruth's presence.

Myfanwy lay in my place. I crept away shaking uncontrollably and spent the remaining night hours huddled before the dying embers of the fire. Brutus lying at my feet shared my grief.

I was away from home when Ruth died. She and the baby. Myfanwy, sole witness, recited the facts: a litany of circumstance with Ruth losing her balance at the head of the staircase.

The coroner, unmoved by my doubts and fears, believed the child's statement and pronounced a verdict of accidental death.

Dear brother, I knew Ruth, my love, my wife, my comfort had been wrenched from me by guile and malevolence. The ensuing weeks remain a blank with the exception of a cameo of Myfanwy standing in the churchyard separated from me by Ruth's coffin.

I was once again alone torn by grief, reduced to a still greater vulnerability. I decided to leave Myfanwy with a governess and journey to safety and you.

A sudden storm changed my plans. We were soaked returning from the graveyard. I alone dashed for shelter and Myfanwy who chose to remain close to the mound of Ruth's grave, face uplifted to the weeping sky, crooning a rondo with the pagan music of the wind tearing at the black streamers of her hair.

Mrs Bennett nursed me through the weeks of my high fever. Myfanwy, strong as I was weak, wandered at will in and out of my delirium.

I made a slow recovery. It was some time before I was able to resume my evening stroll but what had been a delight to be shared with Ruth and Brutus had degenerated in to a solitary aimless wandering.

Brutus was dead. I'd watched impotent as he sickened and died. My anxiety intensified so rapidly after this disaster that before long I was confined to the curtained safety of my room huddled in a corner. I breathed more easily as darkness fell safer among the shadows.

Long night wanderings failed to tire me as I struggled to break the chains with which Myfanwy held me prisoner.

I'd creep in to the room where she slept and stare at the travesty of what I knew to be the truth. I'd thrust my clenched fists, palms fear-wet, deeper in to the safety of my pockets, fighting my desire to shake her until her spine snapped.

The image of her, dead, head lolling against her chest like some grotesque rag doll, beckoned but the cost of such achievement was touch. I felt unable to pay the price.

I had reached the limit of my endurance.

In the light of that which I have recorded, my dear brother, judging myself to be a reliable witness presenting a true chronicle of events leading to this moment, I would stress I am of sound mind.

Overdosing on laudanum is the final choice of an individual an achievement of defiance and self-assertion against a future without alternatives.

Ruth my dearest love smiles down at me as I begin to die. She comforts me, understanding, applauding the sanity of my action: escape from Myfanwy.

Ten Hours

Dossie Towns felt the warmth of the morning sun as she struggled to move toward the side table. Teeth clenched, she pressed her elbows against the cold tiled bathroom floor but the pain in her leg forced her to give up. Dizzy and breathless ,she attempted to relax. The silent house with the background noise of distant traffic offered no release. She must wait for help until late afternoon, when Allegra was due to pay her weekly visit.

Dossie closed her eyes against the glare of the sun as she drifted into her past.

Allegra, her only child, solemn and serious, always an observer to whom fairies and magic were unimaginable. Today she was to give her summing up in yet another murder case.

Dossie shuddered. Her future might soon be in her daughter's hands.

'Always wear your help button, Mother. It's so easy to fall.' There was no evidence to help her case. It was useless to explain. She had just forgotten to slip it on.

Allegra, black-gowned and bewigged, seemed to stand over her pronouncing the verdict: 'Guilty.'

Dossie felt a shiver of apprehension before making yet another ineffectual attempt to move toward the table. Breathless and exhausted, she faced the reality of a future separation from her bridge friends, her morning coffee group, those companions of her generation with whom she shared the ups and downs of encroaching age.

James, whose strong hands loved so gently, would have

reacted differently. He knew what it was like to be old and forgetful.

The long years of aloneness had been so hard. Memory brought tears which she brushed away impatiently before attempting to move her unresponsive leg.

Pain became agony, forcing her to fight a nausea which threatened to overwhelm. Alone, vulnerable, she sobbed as the midday sun rose higher, catching the roundness of the help button, touching the top of the jacaranda tree seen through the window.

James had planted the seedling when Allegra was born. 'A gift of love,' he had said as he watered the small offering. 'Our tree will grow with our family.'

Sadly, there had been no more babies. Their small circle of togetherness had closed around their years of shared happiness until that dreadful day when James became the victim of a fatal afternoon traffic accident.

'James, James.' Tears blurred her vision as the black moment carried her into the past. She had conquered grief but an aching regret would always be with her.

Selfishly, she had wanted him home early to help celebrate Allegra's birthday: he had been caught in that fragment of time. Nothing brought consolation. The price had been everlasting loneliness.

Dossie shivered. Evening shadows were beginning to move across the floor of the bedroom nearby.

Where was Allegra? Surely not another late evening?

She shook her head, attempting to clear her vision. Her strength seemed to have ebbed. Lying in the deepening darkness, she noticed the shadow in a corner. She watched as it seemed to moved closer.

Caught in a sudden memory of the shared love of long ago, she held out her arms. 'James, James,' she sobbed. 'You've come for me at last. I've been waiting for you.'

Poco

Poco Guardia arrived while his mother was on her half-hour break at the family café. She had been peeling vegetables all morning when she felt the need of a bathroom visit. So it was that he came head first, straight into the toilet bowl. The new baby was placed immediately into the closest drawer, which happened to hold the paper serviettes: midday was a busy time and Mia Guardia had a strong work ethic.

Poco (little gift) was a contented baby. Mia possessed an abundance of milk and love but he remained underweight as seen against his brown-eyed, curly-haired cousins.

'My little changeling,' Mia crooned as she nursed her green-eyed, auburn-haired son, warming his long fingered hands between her work roughened palms.

When he was a youngster, the fact that there was no male parent in his life did not worry Poco, as he was not considered to be odd man out among his childhood friends. He did often question his mother, but she became so agitated he was forced to stop.

The situation was not improved when it was discovered that he had asked the local red-haired priest if he was his father.

After that episode, Poco wove his own picture of a dream parent: strong and handsome, eyes green with a shared unusual brown fleck, possessed of a deep love for his son, somehow trapped in a situation which meant he was unable to recognise his little family

Poco made the decision that changed his life and surprised his family when he was a young teenager. Having accepted the fact that he was never going to solve the mystery of his missing parent, he decided to make his mother proud of him.

His early years had been spent helping in the café, readying him for his future. Now Poco became an excellent student. The reward of all those late nights spent in extra revision was a scholarship to university.

Seven years later, he graduated as a doctor. It was not an unexpected move when he chose to become an eye surgeon. Poco, hopeful, always unsuccessful, looked for that unusual brown fleck in any green-eyed patient who passed through his consulting rooms.

At fifty, he noticed the first signs of an unusual macular degeneration. All treatment was unsuccessful. Strong light became so painful he was forced to give up his practice and wear dark glasses which blurred his vanishing vision.

The long empty days were spent in an isolation so intense he became almost despairing, more so when his mother, who had always delighted in his success, passed away.

The suggestion that he take part in a new treatment seemed a lifeline. The small group who gathered in the far-off city hospital set in beautiful gardens, were all in different stages of the experiment. Poco, the newcomer, saw his companions as featureless blurs. Some, further ahead in the course, no longer needed dark glasses.

Long hours between treatments and group meetings were spent in the gardens, much of it sharing memories of their early lives.

So it was that Poco told of his unsuccessful searching for his absent father.

A slightly built, elderly, bald-headed man, first to be given the new treatment, almost ready to return to his village, spoke of his life. In his youth, a landscape gardener to a large group of estates, he travelled widely, holding consultations over several weeks at a time. There had been a girl he had met and hoped to marry but he had been involved in an accident which had left him with devastating loss of memory. Sadly he shook his head, wiping away tears as he murmured, 'If only my memory of that time so long ago would return completely.'

Poco leant forward. Gently he placed his hand round the old man's shoulder. 'It's hard, isn't it?' He sighed deeply. 'The constant lack of success. The driving need to never give up trying.'

Stress tightened the old man's lined features. 'That young girl, my love. Such hurt and shame she must have suffered.'

Poco felt a sudden rush of sympathy. 'Maybe one day you will regain your memory of those times. There's always hope.'

Green eyes flecked with brown widened with surprise. 'I have the strangest feeling I should know you.' He slapped the side of his head with one long-fingered hand. 'Sorry about that.'

The Obsession of Mr Brooks

When Mr Brooks retired, he became a weed addict. One knee bent, with white bowed head and scavenging fingers, he used the daylight hours up in endless pursuit of his goal.

Perhaps he set himself a certain quota of buckets to fill every day or was it a certain quota of hours? Maybe he made the decision during breakfast before he collected his implements: a cardboard knee-rest, his bucket and a sharp-pronged garden fork. In his pocket were his pieces of white rag and string with which he staked out his goal for the day.

Caught on a rainy day in the sluggish flow of early morning traffic, the deserted pocket-sized front lawn gave me the impression that the gnome-caricatured statue had been stolen during the night. What did Mr Brooks do on days like this, I wondered as I peered between the fandango of the windscreen wipers. I could not imagine him reading a book or watching television. Did he help Mrs Brooks in the house? More likely he spent the time sitting at the window counting the raindrops until they fell at a lesser pace, enabling him to carry on his vendetta; or did he spend the rainy hours just sitting while Mrs Brooks rubbed his cramped knee and neck muscles back into viability?

My mind wandered back to the days when we had all been much younger and had shared our neighbours' lives to a much greater degree. Childless, they had been inseparable. What did Mrs Brooks do now, I mused. I had not seen her for years but my question was answered as I crept forward with the traffic. Suddenly she appeared, umbrella aloft, in her virginal bowling outfit; her femininity annihilated by some male chauvinist of decades long past.

The sun came out, the temperature in the car rose higher, so I joined those others on the footpath who had realised that it would be some time before the lane was cleared. It was years since I had stood directly outside 'Le Nid'. Strangely, there was no sign of Mr Brooks. I wondered why, but as soon as I looked closely at the lawn, I had the answer. There it lay, beautiful in its pristine cleanliness; not a weed in sight. It was finished. Mr Brooks had completed his reason for living. His future, no doubt, stretched into grey days of nothingness.

It was then that the semi-trailer, fully loaded, turned the corner. The gutter may as well have been non-existent, the fence a piece of cotton as it ploughed devastatingly across the small place. Mrs Brooks's virginity split apart. Drowned in her own blood, she lay sprawled across the bonnet of the monster which stopped a few inches from the brick wall of the house.

Mr Brooks appeared as if by magic.

The driver, stiff with shock, muttered over and over again, 'My God, my God,' while the small space rapidly filled with a gaggle of bystanders: the helpful and those strange people who take their experience of life second-hand.

'She's dead. I am sorry.'

He looked at me with an unusual lift to his shoulders as if from somewhere he had received an elixir which was sending the blood coursing through his veins with the energy of youth.

'Thanks for your sympathy, Mrs Smith.'

His gaze wandered. 'Just look at the lawn. After I get Mum buried, I'll have a real job ahead of me. The whole thing will have to be relaid and before long the weeds will try and take over.' He sighed heavily then smiled. 'I hate weeds,' he said, but I knew he could not live without them.